Miss Daisy Is Still Crazy!

Dan Gutman

Pictures by
Jim Paillot

SCHOLASTIC INC.

To Emily Stevenson
—D.G.

To Lisa, Cam, and Rosie
—J.P.

ISBN 978-1-338-09934-8

Text copyright © 2016 by Dan Gutman. Illustrations copyright © 2016 by Jim Paillot. All rights reserved. Published by Scholastic Inc., 557 Broadway, New York, NY 10012, by arrangement with HarperCollins Children's Books, a division of HarperCollins Publishers. SCHOLASTIC and associated logos are trademarks and/or registered trademarks of Scholastic Inc.

The publisher does not have any control over and does not assume any responsibility for author or third-party websites or their content.

12 11 10 9 8 7 6 5 4 3 2 1   16 17 18 19 20 21

Printed in the U.S.A.   40

First Scholastic printing, October 2016

Typography by Kathleen Duncan

Contents

Toenails Don't Have Brains

My name is A.J. and I hate germs.

Germs are ugly and gross and mean. Germs should be against the law. The police should arrest germs and throw them in jail—little germ jails. That would teach them a lesson.

When I walked into Mr. Cooper's class the other day, all the girls were *ooh*ing and *ahh*ing about something. I peeked to see what they were looking at. It turned out that Andrea Young—Little Miss I-Know-Everything—got a smartphone from her parents.

"Smartphones are cool!" said Emily, Andrea's crybaby friend.

"My mom said I can use it to look things up," Andrea told the girls.

"Why don't you look up how to be less annoying?" I told Andrea.

"Oh, snap!" said my friend Ryan.

"Think of it," Andrea told me. "I have all the information in the world right here in my hand, Arlo."

Andrea calls me by my real name

because she knows I don't like it. She was a real smarty-pants even *before* she got a smartphone. Now she's going to be an even smarter smarty-pants. Why can't a truck full of smartphones fall on her head?*

I put my backpack into my cubby and went to my seat. Then I looked around. Something was missing. What was it?

Oh, yeah, I know. It was our teacher, Mr. Cooper!

"Where's Mr. Cooper?" asked Michael, who never ties his shoes.

"Where's Mr. Cooper?" asked Alexia,

————————————————

*What are you looking down here for? The story is up *there*, dumbhead!

3

this girl who rides a skateboard all the time.

"Where's Mr. Cooper?" asked Neil, who we call the nude kid even though he wears clothes.

In case you were wondering, everybody was asking where Mr. Cooper was.

That's when our principal, Mr. Klutz, walked into the room. He has no hair at all. I mean *none*. He should get a hair transplant from a hairy guy who has plenty of hair to spare.

"Where's Mr. Cooper?" we all asked.

"Mr. Cooper isn't feeling well today," Mr. Klutz told us.

"Gasp!" everybody gasped.

"I hope he's going to be okay," said

Emily, who's always worried about every-body being okay.

"Oh no!" I shouted, just to yank Emily's chain. "Mr. Cooper is gonna *die*!"

Everybody started yelling and scream-ing and shrieking and hooting and hollering and freaking out.

"We've got to *do* something!" shouted Emily, and then she went running out of the room.

Sheesh, get a grip! That girl will fall for *anything*.

"Calm down!" said Mr. Klutz as he went to the whiteboard and picked up a marker. "Mr. Cooper told me he has . . ."

And then Mr. Klutz wrote this big, long word on the board. . . .

ONYCHOCRYPTOSIS

What?!

I couldn't even *pronounce* that word.

"It sounds like a *horrible* disease!" said

Alexia.

"I *told* you Mr. Cooper is going to die!" I shouted.

Everybody started yelling and screaming and shrieking and hooting and hollering and freaking out again.

"I just looked that word up on my smartphone," said Andrea. "It means 'ingrown toenail.'"*

"What's an ingrown toenail?" asked Michael.

"That's when your toenail grows into your skin instead of out," Mr. Klutz explained.

"Yuck!" everybody shouted. "Gross!"

"Why would a toenail want to grow into

---

*The Ingrown Toenails would be a good name for a rock band.

your skin?" I asked.

"Toenails don't *want* to do *anything*," said Neil. "Toenails don't have brains."

Toenails are weird.

"That sounds scary," said Ryan. "What if Mr. Cooper's toenail grows the wrong way, and it grows inside his body until it comes out the top of his head?"

"Ewww!" everybody started shouting. "Disgusting!"

"Relax, that's not going to happen," Mr. Klutz told us. "Nobody has *ever* had a toenail sticking out of their head."

"There's always a first time," I said.

"Is Mr. Cooper really going to die?" asked Alexia.

"Mr. Cooper is super," said Ryan. "He

has superpowers, so he can't die. That's a fact."

"Nobody *ever* died from an ingrown toenail," Mr. Klutz told us.

"There's always a first time," I said again.

Emily came back to class and sat in her seat.

"Okay, everyone calm down, please," said Mr. Klutz. "Mr. Cooper will be back to school tomorrow. He told me he's going to see his doctor this morning. For the rest of the day, you will have a sub."

"Sub sandwiches all day?" I shouted. "Hooray!"

"Not a sub *sandwich*, dumbhead," said Michael. "A sub is a boat that goes underwater. It's a submarine."

I knew that. Submarines are cool. But why would we be getting a submarine all day just because Mr. Cooper has an ingrown toenail? How would a submarine fit inside the classroom anyway?

"Not a *submarine*, dumbheads!" said Andrea, rolling her eyes. "A sub is a substitute *teacher*. Right, Mr. Klutz?"

"That's right, Andrea."

Andrea smiled the smile she smiles to let everybody know that she knows something nobody else knows.

Personally, I'd rather have a sub sandwich. Or a submarine. But it's always great when you have a substitute teacher, because then you don't have to do any work or learn anything. That's the first rule of being a kid.

"Will our substitute teacher be nice?" asked Emily, who always cares about how nice everybody is.

"Oh yes, she's *very* nice," said Mr. Klutz.

"I think you know her already. In fact, here she is now."

And you'll never believe in a million hundred years who poked her head into the door at that moment.

Nobody! It would hurt if you poked your head into a door! Why would anybody want to do that? But you'll never believe who poked her head into the door*way*.

I'm not going to tell you.

Okay, okay, I'll tell you. But you have to read the next chapter. So nah-nah-nah boo-boo on you.

Guess Who

It was Miss Daisy!

"Well, hello again, third graders!" she shouted.

If you read a book called *Miss Daisy Is Crazy!*, you know that Miss Daisy was our teacher last year, when we were in second grade. And if you didn't read that book,

well, you should really read that book right now.

Go ahead, read it. We'll wait here.

So did you read it yet?

Anyway, Miss Daisy used to be our teacher. Then she went and got married to the reading specialist, Mr. Macky. Then they had a baby girl named Jackie Macky. Miss Daisy took time off from teaching to take care of the baby. And now she was back as a substitute teacher.

We all ran over and hugged her.

"Miss Daisy!" shouted Emily.

"Miss Daisy!" shouted Ryan.

"Miss Daisy!" shouted Neil.

In case you were wondering, everybody was shouting, "Miss Daisy!"

"Her name isn't Miss Daisy anymore," said Andrea. "Now it's *Mrs.* Daisy, right?"

Oh, yeah. When women get married, they change their name from Miss to Mrs. Nobody knows why.

"You can call me whatever you like," said Miss Daisy. "Not all women change their name. Some of them keep their old name. And some of them put 'Ms.' in front of their name."

That's weird. Women should make up their mind. But Miss Daisy will *always* be Miss Daisy to me.

"I have to go to a meeting," said Mr. Klutz, who's always going to meetings. "I'll be back in a little while to see how you're making out."

Ugh, disgusting! I'm not making out with anybody.

Miss Daisy took off her coat and hung it in the cloakroom.

"I missed you kids *so* much!" she told us. "You're getting to be so big."

"We missed you, too," said Andrea, who is a big brownnoser. "How is your baby, Jackie Macky?"

Miss Daisy took out her purse and showed us about a million hundred baby pictures.

"Awwwww . . ."

"She's cute!"

"She's *adorable*!"

All the girls were *ooh*ing and *ahh*ing over the pictures. Sheesh, it was just a

baby! They were acting like Jackie Macky was the first baby born in the history of the world.

"Don't you think Jackie Macky is cute, Arlo?" Andrea asked me.

"She looks like Winston Churchill," I replied.

I saw some old guy on TV named Winston Churchill. He looked like a big baby. That's when I realized something. *All*

babies look like Winston Churchill.

"Can she walk?" asked Michael.

"No," said Miss Daisy.

"Can she talk?" asked Neil the nude kid.

"No," said Miss Daisy.

"So what good is she?" I asked.

"Arlo!" said Andrea. "That's mean!"

"Jackie Macky will be walking and talking very soon," Miss Daisy told us. "But I'm a little worried about her. Today is her first time in day care."

"Oh, I'm sure she'll be fine," said Alexia.

"But what if something happens to her?" asked Miss Daisy. "She might fall, or one of the other kids might hurt her. I've never been away from Jackie Macky for more than a few minutes."

"Nothing's going to happen," I assured Miss Daisy. "I was in day care when I was Jackie Macky's age, and look how I turned out."

"You're a mess, Arlo," said Andrea.

"Your *face* is a mess!" I told Andrea.

"Oh, snap!" said Ryan.

Andrea and I stuck out our tongues at each other.

"Enough bickering, you two," said Miss Daisy. "We have a lot to do today. Mr. Cooper left me a list of things you need to learn while he's gone."

Miss Daisy picked up a big pad of paper and showed the list to us.

- *Who invented kitty litter?*
- *Why is the Statue of Liberty green?*
- *How many stomachs does a cow have?*
- *Which planet has the most moons?*
- *What is a footnote?**

Miss Daisy looked at the list for a long time. Then she did the most amazing

---

*You won't find the answer down here.

21

thing in the history of the world. She ripped the list into little pieces!

"Those are ridiculous things to learn," she said. "Do you *really* want to learn stuff today?"

"Yes!" shouted all the girls.

"No!" shouted all the boys.

"What do you want to learn?" Miss Daisy asked.

"I want to learn about science," said Andrea.

"Well, I don't know anything about that," replied Miss Daisy.

"I want to learn math," said Emily.

"Well, I don't know anything about that either," replied Miss Daisy.

"I want to learn about history," said Alexia.

"I can't help you there," replied Miss Daisy.

"I want to learn about current events," said Annette.

"I'm clueless about current events," replied Miss Daisy.

Miss Daisy doesn't know anything about *anything*! She must be the dumbest teacher in the history of the world.

"Is there anything that you *do* know about?" asked Michael.

Miss Daisy thought about it for a long time.

"Yes!" she finally told us. "There is one thing I know a lot about. Bonbons!"

Bonbons are chocolate treats about the size of a large acorn. They're yummy.

"I'll tell you what," Miss Daisy said. "Let's take a break from learning new things. You can have indoor recess for the rest of the day. Instead of learning, we can just sit around eating bonbons."

"Yay!" everybody shouted.

Miss Daisy took some bonbons out of her purse and passed them around. She's the best teacher in the history of the world!

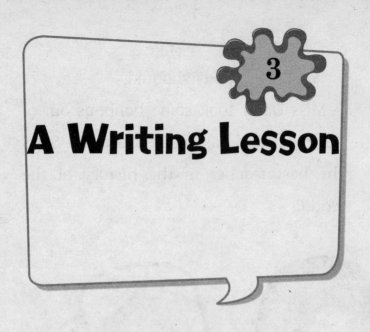

A Writing Lesson

3

We sat around eating bonbons while Miss Daisy kept calling her day care center to see if Jackie Macky was okay. I ate so many bonbons that I got sick to my stomach. It was the greatest day of my life.

Indoor recess is the best. Miss Daisy said we could do whatever we wanted as long as we sat at our desks without talking.

"Can we pass notes to each other?" asked Alexia.

"That's a *great* idea!" said Miss Daisy. "If you kids pass notes back and forth, I can tell Mr. Cooper that we had a writing lesson!"

A few minutes later, a folded-up piece of paper landed on my desk. I opened it, and this is what it said. . . .

U R DUM

I looked around. Michael had a big silly grin on his face, so I knew he was the one who wrote the note. I turned over the paper and wrote this on it. . . .

YOU ARE SO DUMB THAT YOU DON'T EVEN KNOW HOW TO SPELL DUMB!

Then I tossed the note on Michael's

desk. That's when another piece of paper came flying onto my desk from the other direction. I unfolded it, and this is what it said. . . .

A.J. IS A POOPYHEAD

I turned around to see who tossed the note on my desk, but it was impossible to tell. It was probably Ryan, so I wrote RYAN'S MOM EATS WORMS on a piece of paper and tossed it on his desk.

Passing notes is fun. Everybody was writing notes and throwing them on each other's desks. The air was filled with flying notes.

"This is *wonderful*!" said Miss Daisy. "Mr. Cooper will be happy to hear that you kids are working so hard to improve your writing skills."

I picked up a couple of notes that landed next to my desk. One of them said DIARRHEA FACE on it. The other one said STINKY BUTT.

Everybody was passing notes back and forth for a million hundred minutes. After

a while I ran out of silly things to write.

THIS IS BORING, I wrote on a note to Alexia.

WHAT DO YOU WANT TO DO? she wrote back.

I DON'T KNOW, I wrote. INDOOR RECESS IS A DRAG.

I thought I was going to die from boredom. I looked around. Everybody had pretty much finished writing notes. Miss Daisy was still sitting there, eating bonbons and sending texts on her cell phone.

"Miss Daisy," I said, "we're tired of writing notes. Can you teach us something now?"

She came running over to my desk and put her hand on my forehead.

"A.J., are you feeling okay?" she said.

"Maybe you should go to the nurse. I've never heard you say you want to learn something."

"We're bored," said Neil. "Can you teach us about math or something?"

"Math?" asked Miss Daisy. "I hate math! Why do you need to know math? That's why we have calculators."

"But we want to *learn* something," said Andrea.

"Learning things is boring," said Miss Daisy. "Let's just talk. What do you want to talk about?"

"Can we talk about skateboards?" I suggested. Skateboards are cool.

"Yeah," said Alexia. "Let's talk about skateboards."

"Great!" said Miss Daisy. "I *love* skateboarding. Hey, there's something I don't understand about skateboards. Maybe you kids can help me."

"Sure," I said. "I know everything there is to know about skateboards."

"I have these five friends," Miss Daisy told me, "and I bought each of them a skateboard as a present. But the skateboards didn't come with wheels on them. So I have to buy wheels for all my friends. But I don't know how many wheels I need to buy. It's a big problem."

Hmmm, that was a tough one. I had to think about it.

Alexia went over and got a box of glue

sticks from the back of the room.

"Let's say each one of these glue sticks is a wheel," Alexia told Miss Daisy. "A skateboard has four wheels on it, right?"

"I think so," said Miss Daisy. "I'm not sure."

Man, she is dumb!

Alexia took four glue sticks out of the box and put them on her desk.

"And you got skateboards for five of your friends, right?" Alexia asked.

"Exactly."

Alexia took four more glue sticks out of the box and put them on the desk. Those were supposed to be wheels for the second skateboard. Then she did it again for the third skateboard. Then she did it again for the fourth skateboard. Then she did it again for the fifth skateboard. Then we all counted up the glue sticks.

"Four . . . eight . . . twelve . . . sixteen . . . twenty," we all counted.

"You need to get twenty wheels for those skateboards," said Alexia.

"Four times five is twenty," added Andrea.

"That makes sense," said Ryan.

"Hey, wait a minute!" I shouted. "This whole thing sounds a lot like you're giving us a math lesson!"

"No, no, don't be silly!" said Miss Daisy. "We're just talking about skateboards. But I still don't understand why I need that many wheels. Can somebody else explain it to me?"

Neil got a bunch of erasers and put them

on the floor in groups of four to show how Miss Daisy would need twenty wheels for the five skateboards. We spent a million hundred minutes trying to explain it to her. In the end, she *still* didn't get it.

I think Miss Daisy might be the dumbest substitute teacher in the history of the world.

Sound It Out

4

After a while we gave up trying to explain to Miss Daisy why she needed twenty wheels for her skateboards. I'm telling you, that lady is hopeless.

"No worries," she told us. "Let's talk about something else. How about—"

But she didn't get the chance to finish

her sentence. You'll never believe who ran into the door at that moment.

Nobody! It would hurt if you ran into a door. I thought we covered that in chapter 1. But you'll never believe who ran into the door*way*.

It was Mr. Macky, the reading specialist!

"Darling!" Mr. Macky shouted.

"Sweetheart!" Miss Daisy shouted.

Then the two of them ran toward each other and started hugging and kissing.

Ewww, gross! I thought I was gonna throw up.

"Isn't that cute?" said Andrea. "They're in *love*!"

Ugh. Andrea said that four-letter *L* word.

"Do you think Jackie Macky is going to be okay at day care?" Mr. Macky asked Miss Daisy.

"I just called the day care center on the phone," she replied. "Jackie Macky is fine."

"I'm still worried," Mr. Macky said. "Until today she's never been away from us for so long."

"I'm worried, too," said Miss Daisy. "I hope nothing happens to her."

Sheesh! Those two need to take a chill pill.

"As long as I'm here," said Mr. Macky, "does anybody have any questions about reading?"

Little Miss Perfect raised her hand and started waving it around like she was cleaning a giant window.

"Yes, Andrea?"

"I was reading the encyclopedia on my

new smartphone," said Andrea, who actually reads the encyclopedia for fun, "and some of the words were hard to pronounce. What do I do when that happens?"

"Oh, it's simple," Mr. Macky told Andrea. "If you don't understand a word, all you need to do is sound it out. English is a very easy language."

"I tried sounding them out," Andrea said. "But it doesn't always work. Like the word 'right' is spelled *R-I-G-H-T*, but there's also *W-R-I-T-E*. And when I sound it out, I spell it *R-I-T-E*. And that's wrong. So I'm confused."

"Hmmm," said Mr. Macky as he stroked his chin. Grown-ups always say "Hmmm" and stroke their chin when they're thinking. It's the first rule of being a grown-up.

"And what about the word 'through'?" asked Andrea. "If I sound it out, it's spelled *T-H-R-U*. And that's wrong, too."

"Uh, yes," said Mr. Macky. "That's an excellent point. I'll have to get back to you with the answer, Andrea. Does anybody *else* have a question?"

Everybody started shouting out all kinds of questions.

"How come vegetarians eat vegetables, but humanitarians don't eat humans?" asked Ryan.

"How come it's the same thing when an alarm goes off or when an alarm goes on?" asked Michael.

"If the plural of 'tooth' is 'teeth,'" asked Alexia, "how come the plural of 'moose' isn't 'meese'?"

"Wow, look at the time," Mr. Macky said as he pointed to the clock on the wall. "I'd really like to answer those questions for you, but I've got to go . . . uh . . . to a meeting. Yes, that's it. I have a meeting."

Boy, grown-ups sure have a lot of meetings. They meet *all* the time.

"Mr. Macky, why are boxing rings square?" asked Neil the nude kid. "If they're rings, they should be round."

"How come we drive on the parkway and park in the driveway?" asked Michael.

"Why is there no ham in a hamburger and no dog in a hot dog?" asked Ryan.

"How come our noses run and our feet smell?" I asked. "Shouldn't our feet run and our noses smell?"

"Well, this has really been fun," said Mr. Macky as he backed out the doorway. "But I've got to get to that meeting."

"Bye, sweetie pie," said Miss Daisy, running over to him.

"Bye, honey bun," said Mr. Macky.

"I'll see you soon."

"I'll see *you* sooner."

"I love you."

"I love *you* too."

Yuck! Gross! They hugged and kissed some more. That lovey-dovey stuff made me want to barf. All the girls were *ooh*ing and *ahh*ing. All of us guys were gagging and choking and falling off our chairs.

It occurred to me that just like Miss Daisy, Mr. Macky doesn't know anything either! No wonder they got married to each other.

"How can you and Mr. Macky be teachers if you don't know anything?" I asked.

"We figured that kids your age don't

know very much yet," Miss Daisy replied. "So it wouldn't matter whether or not we know anything. Please don't tell Mr. Klutz. If he finds out we don't know anything, he'll fire us."

"My lips are sealed," I told her.

But not with glue or anything. That would be weird.

A few seconds later, guess who came back into our room. It was Mr. Klutz.

"So how are you kids making out with Miss Daisy?" he asked.

"Ugh, gross!" Ryan said. "We're not making out with Miss Daisy."

"But Mr. Macky was," Ryan told him. "They were slobbering all over each other."

"Did Miss Daisy and Mr. Macky teach you all kinds of new things?" asked Mr. Klutz.

"Oh, yeah!" I lied. "They know lots of stuff. They're great teachers."

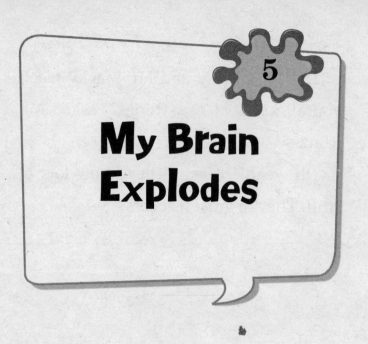

My Brain Explodes

After Mr. Klutz left, Miss Daisy suggested that we have another indoor recess and eat more bonbons. But we were all sick of indoor recess and eating bonbons.

"Can we go out to the playground?" asked Neil.

"No," said Miss Daisy.

"Can we play a game?" asked Alexia.

"No," said Miss Daisy.

"Can I look things up on my smart-phone?" asked Andrea.

"No," said Miss Daisy. "Say, I have an idea. Let's make get well cards for Mr. Cooper!"

"Yeah!" everybody shouted.

Miss Daisy should get the Nobel Prize for that idea.*

Making get well cards is fun. Miss Daisy went to the closet and got some colored paper, crayons, glue sticks, and scissors. She said I could be the paper passer. Ryan was the crayon carrier. Michael was the glue guy. Miss Daisy handled the scissors.

---

*That's a prize they give out to people who don't have bells.

After everybody had their supplies, we got to work on our cards. Miss Daisy said we could write anything we wanted as long as we told Mr. Cooper that we hoped he felt better soon.

"I'm going to draw a picture of butterflies flying over a rainbow on my get well card," said Andrea. "That will cheer up Mr. Cooper."

"Good idea!" said Emily, who thinks all Andrea's ideas are good ideas.

"I'm going to make a picture of a football player," said Neil. "Mr. Cooper likes football, so that will make him feel better."

I thought about what I was going to make for my card. What do you say to somebody who has an ingrown toenail?

I wasn't coming up with any good ideas. I thought and thought for a million hundred minutes. I thought so hard that I felt like my brain was going to explode.

I looked around. Everybody else was busy writing messages and drawing and cutting out pictures to put on their cards.

"Five more minutes," said Miss Daisy. "Let's finish up our get well cards."

I didn't know what to say. I didn't know what to do. I had to think fast. Finally I got an idea and wrote it on my piece of paper. . . .

Dear Mr. Cooper,

I heard you have an ingrown toenail. I hope it doesn't grow so long that it sticks out of your head and you die. I know that's never happened before, but there's always a first time.

Your favorite student,

A.J.

Miss Daisy told us to pass our get well cards to the front of the class. I passed mine up to Andrea.

"Arlo!" she said after looking at my card. "That's not a nice thing to write!"

"Why not?" I asked her. "It's the truth. Should I write that I hope Mr. Cooper's toenail sticks out of his head and kills him?"

Andrea just rolled her eyes at me. She's always rolling her eyes at me. I hope she rolls her eyes so much that her eyes roll right out of her head.

Don't Touch Anything!

After we finished making our cards, Miss Daisy sang the clean-up song. It goes like this. . . .

Clean up! Clean up!
Everybody everywhere.
Clean up! Clean up!
Everybody, do your share.

That song is lame. Of course, the guys and me always change the words. . . .

Clean up! Clean up!
Everybody everywhere.
Clean up! Clean up!
Even in your underwear.

When we finished cleaning up, Miss Daisy said she had a surprise for us—we were going to visit the school nurse, Mrs. Cooney.

Yay! Mrs. Cooney has blue eyes that are the color of cotton candy yogurt. She looks like some movie star, only I can't remember her name. But every time my mom sees that movie star on TV, she asks my dad if he thinks she's pretty. My dad always says no. Then my mom gets mad. Then my dad has to spend the next hour trying to convince my mom that my mom is just as pretty as the movie star.

Mrs. Cooney wanted to marry me last year, but then I found out that she was already married to some guy named Mr. Cooney.

Miss Daisy told us to take our lunch boxes with us, because we would go right to lunch after we saw Mrs. Cooney. Then we had to walk a million hundred miles to the nurse's office. Mrs. Cooney was waiting for us in her nurse's uniform.

"Good morning!" she said.

"Are you going to weigh us and measure us today?" I asked, because she weighs us and measures us every year.

"No, today I'm going to do something much more important," she replied. "Today I'm going to teach you how to wash your hands."

What?!

Was she kidding? I know how to wash my hands. *Everybody* knows how to wash their hands. Teaching us how to wash our hands is like teaching somebody how to breathe through their nose.

But Mrs. Cooney didn't care. She had us all gather around the sink in her office.

"First, you should use warm water," she

said, turning on the faucet. "Next, lather up both sides of your hands with soap. Don't forget your wrists, and between your fingers."

I slapped my own forehead. I couldn't believe that Mrs. Cooney was showing us how to wash our hands.

Andrea was taking notes on her smartphone, of course. She probably thought there was going to be a quiz at the end, or she might win a prize for having the cleanest hands.

"While I'm washing my hands," Mrs. Cooney told us, "I always sing 'Zip-A-Dee-Doo-Dah.' That way I know I'm washing my hands long enough."

She started singing "Zip-A-Dee-Doo-Dah" while she scrubbed her hands.

Mrs. Cooney is loony.

"Finally, rinse off the soap and dry your hands with a clean towel," she told us as she held her hands under the water. "And that's the correct way to wash your hands!"

Well, duh!

Mrs. Cooney had us all line up to wash our hands. She even had Miss Daisy wash *her* hands.

After we all dried off, we sat on the benches in the nurse's office.

"Why is washing our hands so important?" Miss Daisy asked.

"It's all because of germs," Mrs. Cooney told her.

"What are germs?" asked Miss Daisy,

who doesn't know anything.

"Germs are tiny invaders that can make you sick," Mrs. Cooney said. "You can't see them with your naked eye."

Everybody started giggling because Mrs. Cooney said the word "naked." Any time anybody ever says "naked," you have to start giggling. That's the first rule of being a kid.

"Aren't *all* eyes naked?" I asked. "I never saw an eyeball with clothes on."

Everybody laughed even though I didn't say anything funny.

"You need a microscope to see germs," said Mrs. Cooney. "Germs are so small, if you lined up a thousand of them end to end, they could fit across a pencil eraser."

"WOW," we all said, which is "MOM" upside down.

Mrs. Cooney showed us some pictures of scary-looking germs.

"Think about all the things you touched today," she said. "It's easy for a germ on your hand to end up in your mouth or nose. They creep into our bodies, and we don't notice them. Right now there are ninety trillion microbes inside you."

"Gross!" we all said.

"I'm scared," said Emily, who's scared of everything.

"So washing our hands kills the germs, right?" asked Miss Daisy.

"Not exactly," Mrs. Cooney replied. "Plain old soap doesn't kill germs. It just lifts them off your skin so they can be washed away. We can get rid of *some* of the germs but not all of them. And germs multiply very quickly."

Miss Daisy looked really nervous. I thought she might even start to cry.

"Do . . . babies . . . have germs?" she asked.

"Oh yes, babies probably have more germs than *anybody*," said Mrs. Cooney. "Especially babies who like to put their hands in their mouth."

"Jackie Macky sticks her hands in her mouth all the *time*!" shouted Miss Daisy.

"Germs can cause infections," explained Mrs. Cooney. "They can give you sore throats, chicken pox, measles, flu, and lots of other dangerous diseases that can even kill you."

"KILL YOU?" shouted Miss Daisy. She was totally freaking out.

"I don't mean to suggest—"

But Mrs. Cooney didn't have the chance to finish her sentence. Miss Daisy had jumped off the bench and was heading for the door.

"Are there germs on this doorknob?" she shouted.

"Yes, absolutely," said Mrs. Cooney.

"Kids! Don't touch that doorknob!" shouted Miss Daisy. "Are germs on that chair?"

"Sure."

"Are germs in my hair?" shouted Miss Daisy.

"Yes, definitely," Mrs. Cooney replied. "They're even floating in the air."

"EEEEK!" shouted Miss Daisy, swatting

at some invisible germs. "The germs are in the air! They're on the chair! They're in my hair! They're *every*where!"

"We've got to *do* something!" shouted Emily.

"Don't touch anything!" shouted Miss Daisy.

"We're all going to die!" I shouted.

Everybody started yelling and screaming and shrieking and hooting and hollering and freaking out again—again.

"Germs could kill Jackie Macky!" shouted Miss Daisy.

Then she took a tissue, turned the doorknob with it, and went running out of the nurse's office.

It was cool. And we got to see it live and in person with our own eyes.

Well, it would be weird to see it with somebody *else's* eyes.

Germ Warfare

Miss Daisy wasn't the only one who ran out of the nurse's office. We *all* ran out of there.

"Run for your lives!" shouted Neil the nude kid. "The germs are everywhere!"

As we were running out of the nurse's office, the lunch bell rang.

*BRING! BRING! BRING!**

So we all ran to the vomitorium. It used to be called the cafetorium, but last year some first grader threw up in there, and it's been the vomitorium ever since.

Ryan grabbed the last table that was empty. We all opened up our lunch boxes.

I had a peanut butter and jelly sandwich. Alexia had a peanut butter and jelly sandwich. Neil had a peanut butter and jelly sandwich. Emily had a peanut butter and jelly sandwich. In case you were wondering, we all had peanut butter and jelly sandwiches.

---

*The bells in our school sound like the word "bring." Nobody knows why.

But nobody picked up their peanut butter and jelly sandwich.

"I'm not hungry," I said.

"Me neither," said Ryan, who will eat anything, even stuff that isn't food. "Mrs. Cooney said that germs are everywhere."

"Germs are crawling all over our sandwiches right now," said Michael, closing his lunch box. "We can't see them. And we can't stop them."

"The table has germs on it too," said Andrea.

"Your *face* has germs on it," I told Andrea.

"Everybody's face has germs on it," said Emily.

"*Everything* has germs on it," said Neil.

"Everything is gross," I said.

"I'm never going to eat anything ever again for the rest of my life," said Ryan.

"Me neither," said Michael.

So we all just sat there for a million hundred seconds. All the kids at the other tables were eating their lunch. I guess they didn't know about germs.

That's when the weirdest thing in the history of the world happened. Ryan's foot touched my foot.

"Ewww," I told Ryan. "Move your foot. It has germs on it. I don't want your germs!"

"Your elbow almost touched mine," Neil told Alexia.

"I don't *want* to touch you," Alexia replied. "I'm never going to touch anything again."

Nobody wanted to touch anything. I felt gross just sitting there with all those germs crawling all over me. It was the worst day of my life. I wanted to go to Antarctica and live with the penguins. I bet it's so cold there that it kills all the germs.

And you'll never believe who walked into the vomitorium at that moment.

It was Mrs. Cooney! She came right over to our table and put her hand on my shoulder.

Ugh, gross! Her hand was probably covered with germs.

"Mmm," she said, "those peanut butter and jelly sandwiches look *really* good."

"We're not hungry," Michael told Mrs. Cooney. "We're afraid of getting germs."

"That's too bad," Mrs. Cooney replied. "Those sandwiches sure look tasty. It would be a shame if they went to waste."

"You can have my sandwich," said Emily. "I don't want it."

"Sure!" Mrs. Cooney said. Then she picked up Emily's sandwich and took a big bite out of it.

"Ugh!" we all shouted. "Gross!"

"Now you have germs in your *mouth*!" shouted Alexia.

"That's true," said Mrs. Cooney after she finished chewing, "but you kids ran out of my office so fast, I didn't have the chance to finish what I was saying."

"What were you going to say?" asked Andrea.

"I wanted to tell you that most germs won't harm you," said Mrs. Cooney. "Some germs are *good* germs."

"*Good* germs?" we all asked.

"Sure!" said Mrs. Cooney. "There are millions of them."

"The good germs should have a war with the bad germs," I said, "and they should kill them all. It would be a germ war."

"Well, they sort of do that, A.J.," said

Mrs. Cooney. "The good germs help us digest our food, absorb nutrients, and fight disease. In fact, we couldn't live without them. Germs are our friends."

Wow, it would be weird to have a germ as your friend. Germs are so small. What would you do together? I don't think I could play video games with a germ. And I don't think germs know how to ride a skateboard or play football.

"Are there *really* good germs, Mrs. Cooney?" asked Andrea.

"Sure," she replied. "Go ahead and eat your sandwiches. You'll be fine. Hurry up! Lunch is almost over."

After talking with Mrs. Cooney, I felt a lot better. We all wolfed down our sandwiches quickly. I finished mine just before the bell rang.

BRING! BRING! BRING!

It was time to go back to class.

We all rushed down the hall to tell Miss Daisy the news about the good germs.

8

You Can't Be Too Careful

When we got to our class, the weirdest thing in the history of the world happened. Miss Daisy was sitting in Mr. Cooper's chair.

Well, that's not the weird part. People sit in chairs all the time. The weird part is what Miss Daisy was wearing.

It wasn't her regular clothes. She was wearing a bright-yellow baggy suit that covered her whole body. She even had on one of those gas mask things and thick, rubber gloves. She looked like some kind

of weird astronaut or a deep-sea diver.

"Miss Daisy! What's that you're wearing?" asked Alexia.

"It's a hazmat suit," she replied.

Hazmat suit? I never heard of a hazmat suit. *Nobody* ever heard of a hazmat suit.

I was going to ask Miss Daisy what a hazmat suit was, but Little Miss Know-It-All had already looked it up on her smartphone.

"'Hazmat' is short for 'hazardous material,'" said Andrea. "It says here that hazmat suits protect people from chemicals, gases, viruses, and other dangerous airborne particles."

"I don't want to catch any germs," Miss Daisy told us.

"But most germs are *good* germs," Michael explained. "That's what Mrs. Cooney told us."

"I don't care," Miss Daisy said. "If I'm wearing a hazmat suit, I won't get Jackie Macky sick when I get home from school today."

Sheesh, and I thought *my* mother was overprotective.

We put our lunch boxes into our cubbies and sat in our seats.

"Where do you think Miss Daisy got a hazmat suit?" Michael whispered to me.

"From Rent-A-Hazmat Suit," I explained. "You can rent anything."

Miss Daisy stood up and shuffled over to the front of the room. It looked like it was hard to walk in the hazmat suit.

"Okay, it's time we did some learning around here," she said. "What do you want to learn?"

"I want to learn about ancient Egypt," said Andrea.

"Well, I don't know anything about that," replied Miss Daisy.

"I want to learn about the presidents," said Emily.

"Well, I don't know anything about that either," replied Miss Daisy.

"I want to learn about weather," said Alexia.

"Now *that's* something I know about!" said Miss Daisy excitedly.

I couldn't believe it. For the first time in

the history of the world, Miss Daisy was actually going to *teach* us something. She shuffled over to the window.

"If you look outside, you'll see weather,"

she told us. "It's a sunny day today. It's not raining. It's a little chilly. And that's all you need to know about weather."

What?!

That's *it*? That's all she was going to teach us about weather?

"I was watching the Weather Channel once," said Ryan. "They said that clouds are tiny drops of water or ice crystals. They're so light that they float in the air."

"Is that so?" said Miss Daisy. "I had no idea."

"Aren't there different kinds of clouds?" asked Neil. "My dad told me that."

"A cloud is a cloud," said Miss Daisy. "That's all I know about clouds. You see one cloud, you've seen 'em all."

Little Miss Perfect, of course, was all over her smartphone.

"It says here there are four main types of clouds," said Andrea. "Cirrus, nimbus, stratus, and cumulus."

"Cumulus clouds are those puffy ones that look like cotton balls," said Alexia.

"I knew that," said Emily.

"Me too," said Neil.

"Wow, I didn't know *any* of that," said Miss Daisy. "You kids are so smart! You've taught me a lot today. I'm so glad I decided to go into the field of education."

Miss Daisy truly doesn't know anything about *anything*. I'll never understand how she got to be a teacher.*

At that moment, you'll never believe who ran through the door.

Nobody! You can't run through a door. Doors are made of wood.

But you'll never believe who ran through the door*way*.

It was Mr. Macky! And he was wearing a hazmat suit, too!

"Angel muffin!" yelled Miss Daisy.

"Sugar plum!" yelled Mr. Macky.

Ugh, disgusting! I'm sure they would have started hugging and kissing each other if they hadn't been wearing hazmat suits.

---

*I dare you to stand up right now, wherever you are, and scream out, "I love cheese!"

Even though he had a gas mask over his face, we could still tell that Mr. Macky was upset. His eyes looked all crazy.

"What's the matter, dear?" shouted Miss Daisy.

"I just got off the phone with the day care center!" shouted Mr. Macky.

"What happened?" shouted Miss Daisy. "Did Jackie Macky fall down?"

"No."

"Did one of the other kids hit her?"

"No. Jackie Macky has . . ."

We all leaned forward to hear what Jackie Macky had. Everybody was on pins and needles.

Well, not really. We were sitting on chairs. If we were on pins and needles, it would have hurt. But there was electricity in the air.

Well, not really. If there was electricity in the air, we all would have been electrocuted.

But we really really *really* wanted to know what Jackie Macky had.

I could tell you right now what Jackie Macky had. But I'm not going to. You have to read the next chapter to find out. So nah-nah-nah boo-boo on you.

This Is an Emergency!

"Jackie Macky has the sniffles!" shouted Mr. Macky.

What?!

"The sniffles?!" shrieked Miss Daisy. "Oh no! Not the sniffles!"

"Yes, the sniffles!" screamed Mr. Macky. The two of them started jumping up

and down and yelling and screaming and shrieking and hooting and hollering and freaking out. It was hilarious. You should have been there!

"That means Jackie Macky has germs!" hollered Miss Daisy. "Germs have infected her body! And they're going to multiply!"

Wow, I didn't even know that germs could do math. They must be really smart.

"Jackie Macky is sick!" yelled Mr. Macky. "She could die! What are we going to do?"

"Uh, maybe you should wipe her nose with a tissue?" I suggested.

"No!" screamed Miss Daisy. "We need to call an ambulance! This is an emergency! It's a matter of life and death!"

"Right!" shouted Mr. Macky. "You call the ambulance on your cell phone while I drive to the hospital. We can meet them there."

"Good plan, honey!" hollered Miss Daisy. "We have to get out of here. Have a nice day, kids! It was fun teaching you."

"I'm so glad we bought these hazmat suits!" yelled Mr. Macky. "They really came in handy."

Then the two of them ran out of the room.

Teachers are weird. Mr. Macky is wacky. And Miss Daisy is *still* crazy!

Nobody said anything for a million hundred seconds.

"Gee, I hope Jackie Macky is going to be okay," said Emily, who's always wondering if people are going to be okay.

"She has the *sniffles*!" said Alexia. "*Everybody* gets the sniffles. Mr. Macky and Miss Daisy are totally overreacting. My parents did the same thing when my little sister was born."

"What are we going to do *now*?" asked Andrea. "We don't have a teacher."

Andrea was right for once in her life. There were no grown-ups in the room at all. Me and Michael and Ryan looked at each other. Then we snapped into action. The three of us got up and shook our butts at the class.

"Boys!" Andrea said, rolling her eyes.

"I guess Mr. Klutz will have to get another sub for our class," said Emily.

"We're getting sandwiches?" I yelled. "Yay!"

"No, dumbhead!" Andrea said. "Mr. Klutz will have to get another substitute *teacher.*"

Oh. I knew that. I was going to say something mean to Andrea, but I never got the chance. You'll never believe who ran into the doorway at that moment.

I'm not going to tell you.

Okay, okay! I'll tell you. And you don't even have to read the next chapter.

It was Mr. Cooper!

10

Feet Are Disgusting

"Have no fear, CooperMan is here!"

Mr. Cooper came running into the room like he was trying to catch a bus. As usual, he tripped over the garbage can, banged into a desk, and went flying into the whiteboard before falling on the floor.

"Oww!" he yelled. "My toe!"

We all ran over to him.

"Are you okay?" everybody was asking.

"Of course!" Mr. Cooper said as we helped him up. "Neither snow nor rain nor heat nor foot problems can prevent me from educating the youth of America!"

"We heard about your ingrown toenail," said Andrea.

"Yes, it was pretty serious," Mr. Cooper told us. "I was afraid it was going to grow inside my body until it came out the top of my head. But I used my superhealing powers to recover quickly."

"Can we see your toe?" I asked.

"Sure!" Mr. Cooper replied.

He rolled up his pants.

Then he took off his shoe.

Then he took off his sock.

Ugh! It was disgusting. Feet are gross even when you have *normal* toes. Everybody was gagging. I thought I was gonna throw up.

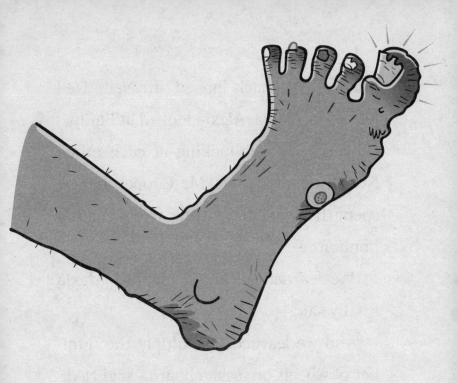

"So, what did you learn while I was out today?" Mr. Cooper asked as he put his sock back on.

We didn't learn *anything*, of course, because Miss Daisy doesn't know anything. I looked at Ryan. Ryan looked at

Michael. Michael looked at Neil. Neil looked at Alexia. Alexia looked at Emily.

Everybody was looking at each other. Nobody wanted to tell Mr. Cooper that we spent the whole day sitting around eating bonbons.

"We learned all about clouds," Alexia finally said.

"And we learned to multiply the number of wheels on a skateboard," said Neil.

"And we learned about germs," said Michael.

Hmmm. Come to think of it, we did learn a lot of stuff.

"Wonderful! Now, where's that list of questions I left you?" asked Mr. Cooper.

"There were some other important things I wanted you to learn today."

Nobody wanted to tell Mr. Cooper that Miss Daisy ripped up his list and said it was ridiculous.

"Oh, I took a picture of your list with my smartphone," Andrea finally said, taking

out her phone. "We did some research."

"And what did you find out?" asked Mr. Cooper.

"Kitty litter was invented by a man named Ed Lowe in 1947," Andrea read from her notes. "Jupiter has the most moons. The Statue of Liberty turned green because of chemical reactions between the copper coating and water. Cows have four stomachs. And a footnote is some words at the bottom of a page that explain something above it."

Wow! When did Andrea have the time to look all that stuff up?

"Very good, Andrea!" said Mr. Cooper. "I'm glad you didn't waste your time while I was away."

"Oh, I never waste time, Mr. Cooper!"

Andrea smiled the smile she smiles to let everybody know that she knows something nobody else knows. What is her problem?

"Fantastic!" Mr. Cooper said, clapping his hands. "Now let's get back to work! Turn to page twenty-three in your—"

But Mr. Cooper didn't have the chance to finish his sentence, because at that moment the most amazing thing in the history of the world happened.

BRING! BRING! BRING!

It was three o'clock! Time for dismissal! Yay!

When I got home, my parents asked me what happened at school during the day.

"Nothing," I replied.

Any time your parents ask you what happened at school during the day, always say "Nothing." That's the first rule of being a kid.

I sure hope that Jackie Macky recovers from the sniffles. Maybe the police will start to arrest germs and put them in jail. Maybe a truck full of smartphones will fall on Andrea's head. Maybe everybody will start wearing hazmat suits to school. Maybe Mr. Cooper's ingrown toenail will come out the top of his head. Maybe we'll get to eat sub sandwiches. Maybe women will make up their mind and stop changing their name for no reason. Maybe the good germs and the bad germs will start a germ war. Maybe babies will stop looking like Winston Churchill. Maybe Miss Daisy will buy skateboards with wheels on them next time. Maybe humanitarians will start to eat humans. Maybe our feet will run and our noses will smell, instead of the other way around. Maybe Andrea's eyes will roll out of her head. Maybe I'll sing "Zip-A-Dee-Doo-Dah" the next time I wash my hands. Maybe eyeballs will start to wear clothing. Maybe I'll move to Antarctica to get away from the germs. Maybe we can talk Mr. Cooper into letting us sit around and eat bonbons for the rest of the school year.

But it won't be easy!